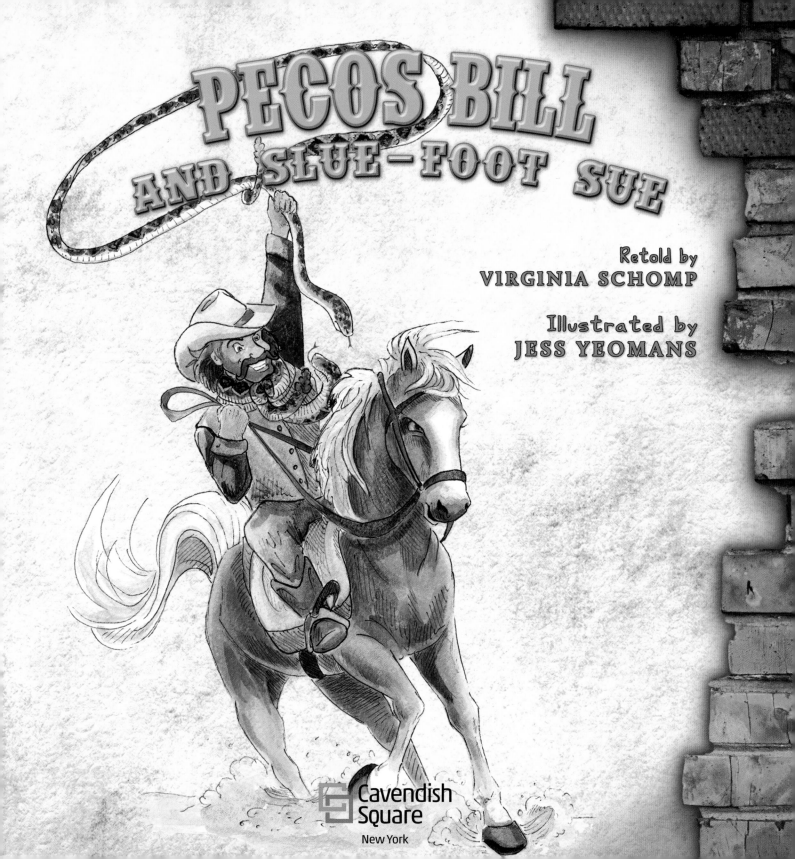

# PECOS BILL
# AND SLUE-FOOT SUE

Retold by
**VIRGINIA SCHOMP**

Illustrated by
**JESS YEOMANS**

Cavendish Square
New York

# HAVE YOU HEARD ABOUT PECOS BILL?

He was the roughest, toughest cowboy in the whole Wild West. He could ride a tornado. He could wallop a mountain lion. He could stop a herd of stampeding cattle with one throw of his rope.

Only one thing ever got the better of Bill—and that was his love for a hard-riding cowgirl called Slue-foot Sue.

3

Pecos Bill was born in east Texas. His parents loved wide-open spaces. When he was a baby, some settlers built a house just fifty miles away. His father cried, "Pack up, Ma! Neighborhood's gettin' crowded!"

So Bill and his sixteen brothers and sisters piled into a covered wagon. The wagon bounced its way across the rocky plains. And round about the Pecos River, little Bill bounced right out.

With so many young'uns, it was three weeks before Bill's folks noticed that he was missing. By then, it was too late to go back. The wagon rolled on west. And poor little Bill was left all alone in the Texas dust.

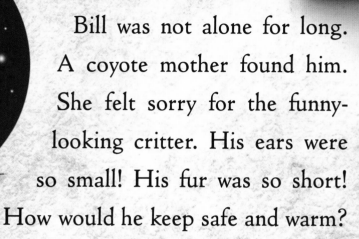

Bill was not alone for long.
A coyote mother found him.
She felt sorry for the funny-
looking critter. His ears were
so small! His fur was so short!
How would he keep safe and warm?
So the mother took the baby home and raised him like
one of her own pups.

Pecos Bill grew up wild and happy. He learned to howl
at the moon. He learned to run, hunt, and fight. He
was faster than the jackrabbit. He was stronger than the
grizzly bear. He was top dog in the
coyote pack and king
of all the critters
in the West.

One day a cowboy came riding along. The man stopped and stared at Pecos Bill. "Where are your clothes, young feller?" he asked.

"I'm not a feller. I'm a coyote, and coyotes don't wear clothes," Bill said.

"If you're a coyote, where's your long, bushy tail?"

Bill looked around at his backside. No tail. Not even a little one. "Well, if that don't beat all!" he said.

And that's how Pecos Bill found out that he was a man. He borrowed some clothes from the cowboy. He howled good-bye to his coyote friends. Then the king of the critters set out to become a cowboy himself.

Pecos Bill ran like lightning across the plains. Suddenly a giant rattlesnake blocked his path. That mean old rattler was itching for a fight. Just to be fair, Bill let it have the first three bites. Then—*WHOMP!*—he knocked the stuffing out of the silly snake and wrapped it around his neck.

A little ways farther, Bill heard a fearsome growl. A huge mountain lion attacked! *THUMP! CRASH! YAHOO!* Bill wrestled the beast to the ground. He squeezed so tight that the big cat meowed like a kitten. Then he slapped a saddle on the mountain lion and hopped up on its back.

Bill rode all the way to Hell's Gate Canyon. The canyon was the hideout of the Hell's Gate Gang. That gang was the toughest bunch of outlaws that ever rode the West.

Bill strolled up to the campfire. He reached into the sizzling kettle and scooped out all the beans. He washed them down with a gallon of boiling-hot coffee. Then he wiped his mouth on a hunk of cactus. "Who's the boss around here?" he asked.

The men gaped at the rattlesnake. They gawked at the mountain lion. They goggled at Pecos Bill. "You are!" they said.

13

Now that Pecos Bill had a gang, he was ready to start cowboying. In those days, the cattle business was one sorry mess. To catch a wild Texas longhorn, the cowboys made a circle out of a chain. They put it on the ground. Then they hid behind a cactus. When a cow or bull stepped in the circle, they pulled on the chain. Sometimes it took a whole month to make a single catch!

Bill had a better idea. He tied some rattlesnakes together. He swung his snake rope in the air and let it fly. The loop came down over a whole herd of longhorns. Pecos Bill had invented the lasso!

Bill made lassos out of cowhide for
all his men. He invented branding, so
they could mark each cow they caught. He
taught them to stay with the herd day
and night, to keep the cattle from wandering.
He even invented cowboy songs. Now the
men could sing the herd to sleep on
the long cattle drives.

16

Pretty soon, Pecos Bill had the world's biggest ranch. It took all of Texas, New Mexico, and Arizona to hold his gigantic herds. At first, it was hard to find enough water for all those animals. But Bill solved that problem. He dug out a new water hole. He called it the Rio Grande—the "Big River."

Bill's mountain lion was not a good cow pony. Whenever it saw a cow, it thought about lunch. Bill needed a real horse. When he heard about Widow-Maker, he knew he had found just the one.

Widow-Maker was a wild stallion. He was faster than lightning. Many men had tried to capture him. No one could even get close. But Bill was no ordinary man. Quick as a coyote, he leaped onto Widow-Maker's back. The stallion twisted and bucked. He raced all the way from Mexico to Canada and back again. Finally, he got tired of running. From then on, Pecos Bill and Widow-Maker were the best of friends.

19

One afternoon, a tornado roared into Texas. The cowboys ran for their lives. Pecos Bill just tossed his lasso. He caught the twister by the throat. He flew up into the air. "Yippee!" he yelled. "This is even more fun than riding Widow-Maker!"

Now the tornado was really mad! It spun faster and faster, trying to throw that crazy cowboy. Bill yanked on his rope. He pulled so tight that the twister cried like a baby. Before long, the tornado cried itself out. Bill slid down to the ground on a lightning bolt. He landed so hard that he made a big hole in California. Today we call that hole Death Valley.

Sometimes Bill liked to ride along the Rio Grande. It was there that he saw an amazing sight. A pretty red-haired cowgirl was riding down the river on the back of a giant catfish! The fish was rearing and bucking. The girl was whooping and hollering. Bill's heart began a-thumping like a herd of runaway cattle.

"Howdy," the cowgirl shouted. "My name is Slue-Foot Sue. I can ride anything that walks, crawls, or swims. I sure would like to ride that stallion!"

"I'm Pecos Bill," said Bill. "I'm the king of the cowboys. I promise to let you ride Widow-Maker—if you will marry me first!"

Pecos Bill and Slue-Foot Sue got married
the very next day. Sue wore a fancy wedding
gown with a bustle. (A bustle was a springy
wire frame that ladies wore under
their skirts to poof them out.) Bill
was so proud when the preacher
said, "I now pronounce you
cowboy and cowgirl."

Then disaster struck. Sue reminded Bill of his promise. She wanted to ride Widow-Maker! She climbed into the saddle, and the horse began to buck. He bucked so hard that Sue flew up in the sky. She landed on her bustle and bounced back up again. Up and down. Up and down. That poor girl bounced so high she nearly hit her head on the moon!

WEDDINGS

Some folks think that Slue-Foot Sue is still bouncing. Others say that Bill caught her with his lasso—only he got yanked up into the sky, too! Some nights, you can see them riding across the heavens on the back of a shooting star.

But most folks tell a different tale. They say that
Bill lassoed Sue and pulled her back down to earth.
They rode off together into the west Texas desert.
There they raised a bunch of young'uns as wild and free
as themselves. Have you ever heard the wind howling like a
pack of coyotes? That just might be Pecos Bill's
family singing to the moon!

# ABOUT PECOS BILL

The cowboys of the Old West were hardworking men. From sunup to sundown, they lived in the saddle. At night, they sat around the campfire. They swapped songs and stories. Each man tried to tell the "tallest" tale, with the boldest hero performing the most amazing deeds.

In the early 1900s, a writer named Edward O'Reilly brought all these tall tales together in the story of Pecos Bill. Bill's adventures teach us about the qualities that mattered most to the men and women of the Old West. He is strong and brave. He is smart and self-reliant. And he can ride out any storm with a smile.

*Our story of Pecos Bill is based mainly on tall tales collected by James Cloyd Bowman for the book* Pecos Bill: The Greatest Cowboy of All Time *(1937) and on the original story by Edward O'Reilly, first published in* The Century Magazine *(1916) and reprinted in the book* Saga of Pecos Bill *(1923).*

# WORDS TO KNOW

**canyon**  A deep, narrow valley with steep sides.

**cattle**  Cows and bulls.

**coyote**  A North American animal that looks like a small wolf.

**lasso**  A long rope with a loop on one end, used for catching animals.

**longhorn**  A type of cattle with very long horns.

**Rio Grande**  A river that forms part of the border between Texas and Mexico. *Rio Grande* is Spanish for "Big River."

**tall tale**  A funny, exaggerated story. Tall tales are unbelievable, but they are told as if they were true.

# TO FIND OUT MORE

**BOOKS**

Balcziak, Bill. *Pecos Bill*. Minneapolis, MN: Compass Point Books, 2003.

Gleeson, Brian. *Pecos Bill*. Rowayton, CT: Rabbit Ears Books, 2005.

Krensky, Stephen. *Pecos Bill*. Minneapolis, MN: Millbrook Press, 2007.

## Videos/DVDs

*Between the Lions: Pecos Bill Cleans Up the West*. Boston: WGBH
Boston Video, 2005.

*Shelley Duvall's Tall Tales and Legends: Pecos Bill.*
Port Washington, NY: Koch Vision, 2005.

## Websites

*American Folklore: Pecos Bill*

www.americanfolklore.net/pecosbill.html

Storyteller S. E. Schlosser retells seven tall tales, including "Pecos
Bill Rides a Tornado" and "Pecos Bill and Slue-foot Sue."

*Pecos Bill: An American Tall Tale*

www.manythings.org/voa/stories/Pecos_Bill.html

Click on the arrow at the top of the page to hear storyteller
Barbara Klein read a rollicking story about Pecos Bill.

## ABOUT THE AUTHOR

**VIRGINIA SCHOMP** has written more than seventy books for young readers on topics including dinosaurs, dolphins, American history, and ancient myths. She lives among the tall pines of New York's Catskill Mountain region. She enjoys hiking, gardening, watching old movies on TV and new anime online, and, of course, reading, reading, and reading.

## ABOUT THE ILLUSTRATOR

**JESS YEOMANS** was born and raised on Long Island, New York, and grew up with a love of art and animals. She received her Illustration BFA at the Fashion Institute of Technology. She has been featured in many exhibits and has been awarded numerous awards and honors for her artwork.

Jess works as a freelance illustrator in Brooklyn. She enjoys drawing and painting, snowboarding, animals, cooking, and being outdoors. To see more of her work, visit www.jessyeomans.com.

Published in 2014 by Cavendish Square Publishing, LLC
303 Park Avenue South, Suite 1247, New York, NY 10010

LIBRARY OF CONGRESS CATALOGING-IN-PUBLICATION DATA
Schomp, Virginia.
Pecos Bill and Slue-Foot Sue / retold by Virginia Schomp. — 1st ed.
p. cm. — (American legends and folktales)
Summary: Relates some of the exploits of Pecos Bill, the extraordinary Texas cowboy who was raised by coyotes, rode a mountain lion, used a rattle snake as a rope, and married the fearless Slue-Foot Sue.
Includes bibliographical references.
ISBN 978-1-60870-444-6 (hardcover)  ISBN 978-1-62712-019-7 (paperback)  ISBN 978-1-60870-610-5 (ebook)
1. Pecos Bill (Legendary character)—Legends. [1. Pecos Bill (Legendary character)—Legends.
2. Folklore—United States. 3. Tall tales.]  I. Title.
PZ8.1.S3535Pec 2012
398.2097302—dc22
[E]
2010023594

EDITOR: Deborah Grahame-Smith
ART DIRECTOR: Anahid Hamparian    SERIES DESIGNER: Kristen Branch

Printed in the United States of America